Text copyright © 2021 by Kirin Hayashi
Illustrations copyright © 2021 by Chiaki Okada
Translation copyright © 2024 by Avery Fischer Udagawa
All rights reserved.

No part of this book may be reproduced, or stored in a retrieval system, or transmitted in any form or by any means, electronic, mechanical, photocopying, recording, or otherwise, without express written permission of the publisher.

Previously published as *Akai Tebukuro* by Komine Shoten Co., Ltd., in Japan in 2021. English translation rights arranged with Komine Shoten Co., Ltd. through Japan Foreign-Rights Centre. Translated from Japanese by Avery Fischer Udagawa. First published in English by Amazon Crossing Kids in collaboration with Amazon Crossing in 2024.

Published by Amazon Crossing Kids, New York, in collaboration with Amazon Crossing

www.apub.com

Amazon, Amazon Crossing, and all related logos are trademarks of Amazon.com, Inc., or its affiliates.

ISBN-13: 9781662516764 (hardcover)
ISBN-13: 9781662516757 (eBook)

The illustrations were rendered in pencils and colored pencils.

Book design by Liz Casal
Printed in China

First Edition
10 9 8 7 6 5 4 3 2 1

TWO LITTLE RED MITTENS

words by **KIRIN HAYASHI**   pictures by **CHIAKI OKADA**
translation by Avery Fischer Udagawa

amazon crossing kids

Two little red mittens.
Left and right, they always went out as a pair,
wrapping Little One's hands in their fluffy warmth.

When Little One pressed and pressed
the pure white snow into snowballs,
the mittens helped.

The first time Little One made a snowman,
the mittens helped.

Every night, drying out by the woodstove, the two mittens promised each other:

"Let's keep those tiny fingers toasty warm tomorrow, and the next day, and the next."

One day, Little One lost the right mitten.
A fox crossing the road spotted it.
"A human child must have dropped this," he said.
He gently hung it on a branch for the owner to find.

But the right mitten was not by the woodstove that night.
Only the left mitten made it home.
It was terribly lonely!

Overnight, a blizzard howled and blew snow all around. The right mitten got knocked off the branch and fell beneath a tree. Just as it was about to be buried in the snow, a passing mother rabbit scooped it up and carried it into the forest.

The next day, as soon as Little One woke up, she searched high and low for the lost right mitten. But it was nowhere to be seen.

Little One went back and forth, back and forth over yesterday's path, and even looked beneath her favorite fir tree, but the mitten was gone.

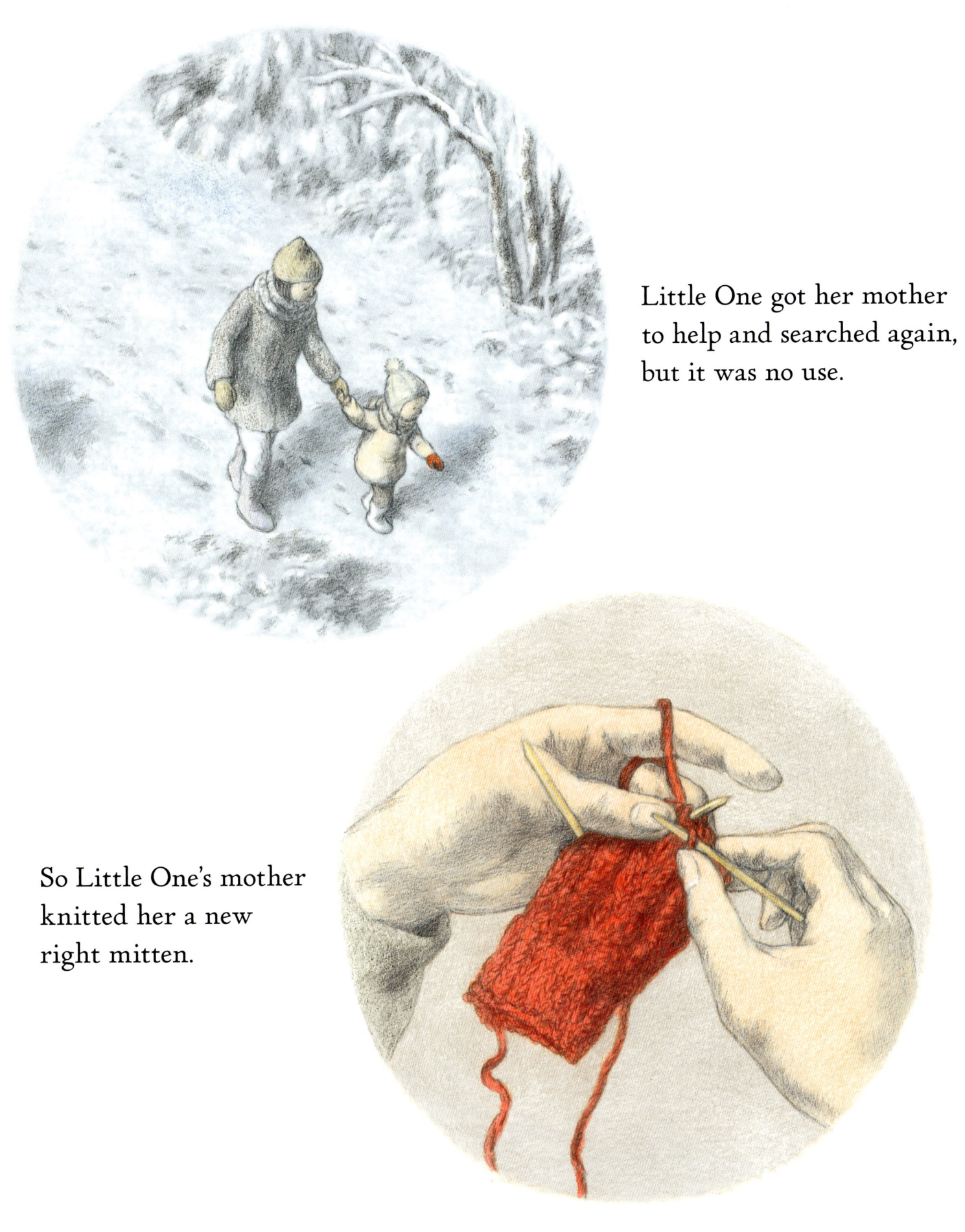

Little One got her mother to help and searched again, but it was no use.

So Little One's mother knitted her a new right mitten.

At the same time, the mother rabbit
was enjoying a cup of hot tea.
It was her favorite kind, made from the many
dandelions she had picked in the spring.
The mitten made the perfect tea cozy.

The mother's twin children came bouncing in.
"Mommy, what's that fluffy red thing?"
"Is that a hat?"
The bunnies drew close together,
cheek to cheek, and pulled the mitten
over both their heads at once.

"How warm . . . It even covers my ears all the way!"
"It's so soft on my forehead!"
The bunnies realized that the mitten made
a perfect nightcap.

Some nights, as the twins were having sweet dreams, the right mitten would lie awake thinking of the left mitten.
What is that mitten up to these days?
The left mitten had always been there.
Even at night, the dear friend had been there.

One day, three little mice came over to play.
When the bunnies showed them their downy red hat,
the mice instantly wanted it for themselves.

They begged and begged, and they wouldn't let go.
Soon, everyone was tugging and yanking.
"Stop! Don't pull!"
"It'll rip!"
At this rate, the mitten would tear in half! The twin bunnies decided to let go, and they gave the mitten away.

The mice hoisted the mitten onto their
shoulders and set off for home.
When they put their heads together
to wear the hat like the bunnies,
it slid right down over their bodies.
How soft and full and light it was!

The three mice, who had trouble
staying still when they slept, had a good idea.
"Let's make it our sleep sack!"
"Yes!"
"Let's!"

And, starting that night,
not one of them stuck out of the covers.
They all slept together,
warm and snug until morning.

As time passed, though, each of the mice
began wanting to sleep alone in the sack.
It would feel so good to have the *whole* thing . . .
and even better on the sunny top of the tree stump!
They each tried to be the first to burrow inside,
and they scuffled and struggled.
They pulled so hard that when they let go,
the mitten zoomed to the top of a bush.

A pigeon spotted it and swooped down.
"Doesn't this look airy and warm! I'll take it home for a blanket."
Clasping it in her beak, the pigeon prepared to fly high.
But then, the bush shook as a long shadow shifted.

"Oh no—a wolf!" The pigeon dropped the mitten and fled to the sky.

But the shadow that had moved was no wolf.
A squirrel came out from beneath the bush and stopped short.
A fluffy red thing was floating down from the sky.
"Is this a gift from the clouds?"

The mitten was frayed and full of holes,
but when the squirrel popped it on,
it was like a pillowy sweater.
"How lovely and comfy!"
The squirrel immediately adored it.

All this time, the left mitten
was working with the new right mitten,
warming and protecting Little One's hands.
Together, they made a big snowman
and brushed the snow off the dog.

With each touch of the pure-white snow,
the left mitten thought of the old right mitten.
I wonder if everything's all right.
They had made tiny snowballs together.
That mitten had helped pull the sled for Little One
and pick up the red berries that fell in the snow.

One day, the left mitten
spied something red on a tree branch.
It looked like a single red flower blooming in the snowy woods.
On second look, it was the old right mitten!
It was stretched, torn, unraveling, and a totally different shape,
but there was no mistake.

The right mitten saw the left mitten too.

Just then, the squirrel came out and
caressed the right mitten with its cheek.

"Ah, it's dry!
I can smell the sun.
Spring is coming, bit by bit!"

The squirrel held the mitten close, treasuring it.

There, in the warm sunlight,
the two mittens passed each other—
the right and the left.
Now they were both very happy.